WATERMELONS, WALNUTS
AND THE WISDOM OF ALLAH

BY BARBARA WALKER

ILLUSTRATED BY HAROLD BERSON

WATERMELONS, WALNUTS AND THE WISDOM OF ALLAH

AND OTHER TALES OF THE HOCA

Parents' Magazine Press

OTHER BOOKS BY BARBARA WALKER
Just Say Hic!
Hilili and Dilili
Stargazer to the Sultan

For my husband, tireless companion
in the search after folktales worth sharing

CONTENTS

INTRODUCTION

In Turkey several hundred years ago, there lived a certain *Nasreddin Hoca* (pronounced Nahz-*red*-din Hoe-djah). In his town of Akshehir, in south-central Turkey, the Hoca served as religious teacher, as Moslem priest, and even occasionally as judge in local disputes. But, like the rest of us, Nasreddin Hoca was entirely human, and that human part of him was what made this particular hoca so appealing. For sometimes, trying to be very wise, he was foolish; and sometimes, seeming to be foolish, he was in truth very wise. Above all, he had the useful gift of being able to laugh at his own mistakes, a trait which has made Turkish children and their parents love him all the more.

When I was living in Turkey, I heard a great many tales about Nasreddin Hoca. Curiously, I heard these tales quite by accident, for they were told to me to illustrate some point the speaker was making. For example, while I was recovering from an illness, I asked my Turkish doctor how long it would take before I should be well enough to travel by ship. Instead of answering my question, he replied, "There's a Nasreddin Hoca story which will answer that question better than I can," and he told me "How Long Will It Take?" For there is a Hoca tale to fit almost any human situation, and the Hoca's wit and wisdom do indeed illuminate the problems and perplexities of everyday life.

Who has not indulged in a bold bit of braggadocio, only to find himself held to his boast? And who therefore could fail to appreciate "The Hoca and the Candle" and "Nasreddin Hoca and the Third Shot"? Who among us, on receiving a punishment too heavy for the "crime," would not value the closing scenes in "Tell Me, When Will I Die?" Who, having received a puzzling answer to a prayer or a request, would fail to enjoy "Cow or Donkey?" And which of us could argue with the Hoca's conclusion in "Watermelons, Walnuts and the Wisdom of Allah"? These and other Hoca tales are here for your delight.

10

Of all Turkish products, they are the most lasting exports. And one who has laughed with the Hoca will learn to love the Turkish folk through whose humor and resiliency Nasreddin Hoca has become a true folk hero.

Nasreddin Hoca lived, we are told by some authorities, during the reign of Tamerlane, for that ruthless ruler appears as a figure in many Hoca tales. He may have lived then, or earlier, or later. What matters most is that he is very much alive today, not only in Turkey but in every other spot on earth fortunate enough to possess even a handful of his tales. Clever fellow that he was, he designed his grave with a gate but no walls, so he can move about as freely as the rest of us.

And I, for one, am glad, for we need all we can find of such kindly men.

Barbara K. Walker

Lubbock, Texas
Christmas Day , 1966

TELL ME, WHEN WILL I DIE?

ONE day as the Hoca was intent on the business of chopping off a rotted limb from his apple tree, the new schoolmaster came along.

"I say, Hoca *effendi*, if you do not take care, you will fall and hurt yourself," he called.

"Oh?" The Hoca rested a moment from the warm job. "How, then, do you know I will fall? Are you a fortuneteller?"

"No, indeed," answered the young teacher. "But any man who sits on the outside end of a branch he is chopping is certain to fall."

13

"Thank you, young man," said the Hoca. "It may be that you know *books*, all right. But I have been cutting trees since long before you were born. I think I can manage this one by myself."

"As you will, Hoca *effendi*," and the schoolmaster walked off down the road toward the coffeehouse.

Just as the last bit of dust had settled to the road behind the schoolmaster's heels, the Hoca gave a great *thwack* with his axe, and the branch broke free. As it fell, so, alas, did the Hoca.

"Big head, big headache!" muttered the Hoca to himself, rubbing the lump swelling under his turban.

Suddenly a startling thought occurred to him, and he ran with robe a-flap down the road toward the coffeehouse. Coming upon the schoolmaster, he gasped, "I say, young man, wait for a moment!"

The schoolmaster stood patiently until the Hoca had caught his breath.

"Many will show me the road once my cart has overturned," began the Hoca. "But you pointed the way before I knew my need. You must indeed be a fortuneteller. Tell me, I pray, when will I die?"

"How should *I* know, Hoca *effendi?*" replied the young man.

"Ah, but you *do* know," insisted the Hoca. "Anyone who can tell me when I am going to fall can *surely* tell me when I am going to die!"

Thinking only to humor the Hoca, the schoolmaster said, "Well, if you must know, Hoca *effendi*, you will die when your hands and feet turn cold and have no feeling."

"Thank you. Thank you!" cried the Hoca. "And may Allah give you a long life." And he hurried back down the road to tell his wife the news.

A few days later, as the Hoca was coming in from his vineyard, he felt a decidedly odd tingling in his fingers and his toes. Was it—could it be . . . ? He was not left long in doubt, for shortly both his hands and his feet became cool, and then cold as marble. "*Ey, vah!*" grieved the Hoca. "It is just as the schoolmaster predicted. I am about to die! I must hurry home and make ready for my funeral."

His poor wife could scarcely believe her ears when the Hoca declared he was about to die. As she stood there wringing her hands and weeping, the Hoca tottered over to his sleeping mat on the floor. "Come, come, my dear. Weep not for the dead, but for the living. Wash me well and prepare my body for

burial. Then call in the neighbors, and they will bring the village coffin and bear me to the cemetery."

In due time, the Hoca was washed and suitably dressed for burial. In came four neighbors with the village coffin, in which the body of the Hoca was placed. Then off they went toward the cemetery, with more and more friends joining the procession as it passed through the village. Every few meters, the pallbearers were replaced by other friends and neighbors who wished to win merit for themselves in the next world by bearing one of Allah's faithful servants to his grave.

Shortly before they arrived at the cemetery, they came to a crossroads. Abruptly they stopped, and a great discussion developed over which road they were to take to reach the Hoca's plot in the graveyard.

"I say we should take *this* one," said the *beckche*, the village watchman, waving his hand toward the road to the left.

"And *I* say we should take *this* one," insisted the storekeeper, waving his hand toward the road to the right. "This road is less muddy."

The discussion moved rapidly toward bitter argu-

18

ment, and voices rose and tempers flashed over the issue. Finally the Hoca roused himself and sat up drowsily. "While I was living," he said slowly, "I always used to go *that* way," pointing to the left. Then he lay down again in the coffin.

The villagers, long accustomed to heeding the Hoca's wise words, took the road to the left, and within a few minutes had removed the Hoca's body from the coffin and deposited the remains reverently in the freshly dug grave. The short service having been conducted with proper respect for the Hoca's position in the community, the mourning procession

returned to the village, leaving the Hoca to the silence of the cemetery and to a quiet mulling over of his untimely death.

Just as the silence had begun to bear in upon the Hoca uncomfortably, there was a tinkling of caravan bells. As the caravan came closer, the Hoca shook off the dirt from the grave and sat up to look. A group of pottery salesmen had taken a short cut through the cemetery, their mules laden with pots and vases and plates of all sorts.

This was too much! Imagine the indecency of using the cemetery as a short cut for mules! The Hoca stood up indignantly to confront the peddler leading the small caravan. But, alas, as he arose from the grave, the mules took fright and, kicking

21

up their heels, took flight for their lives, scattering pottery in all directions. Unable to catch the runaway mules, the peddlers unleashed their wrath on the Hoca, the unwitting cause of their distress. They beat him until he was black and blue from nose to toes, and at last they left him for dead in his own grave.

By this time, the Hoca had had all he could stomach of death. Aching in every bone and muscle, he crept out of the grave and hobbled slowly toward the village. At length, he arrived at the coffeehouse, where he stopped to refresh himself before he stumbled on home. And the village men gathered about him eagerly.

"I say, Hoca," said one. "You've been dead and buried. Tell me, how are things in the next world?"

"Well," replied the Hoca, weighing his words carefully, "everything is fine there, except that you must be careful not to frighten the potters' mules!"

This tale is so well known in Turkey that anyone whose innocent action brings down a punishment entirely out of scale with the offense is said to have "frightened the potters' mules."

SHOES FOR A JOURNEY

NE day when Nasreddin Hoca was just a boy, his friends decided to play a trick on him. After considerable discussion, they agreed to steal his shoes. But how? Suddenly the leader among the group had an idea.

"Nasreddin!" he called.

And Nasreddin obligingly came over to see what was wanted.

"We've been talking, and Ahmet thinks you can climb that cypress tree. Mehmet and I are sure you cannot. Irfan, here, isn't sure whether you can or you can't. What do you say? Can you? Or can't you?"

Nasreddin looked at the tree. Then he looked at his friends. Clearly something besides the tree-climbing was on their minds, but Nasreddin couldn't be sure just what it was.

"Oh, I can *climb* it, all right," he answered.

"Let's see you, then," said the leader. "Here, I'll hold your shoes for you while you climb."

Aha! So *that* was it . . . Shrugging his shoulders, Nasreddin stuffed his shoes into the pockets of his baggy trousers. With a twinkle in his eye, he replied, "I'll just take them along with me. It may be that I'll find a road at the top of the tree. In that case, I shall need my shoes!"

WATERMELONS, WALNUTS, AND
THE WISDOM OF ALLAH

ONE day as the Hoca was working in his little garden, he became very warm. Seeing no one about, he slipped off his turban to cool his head a trifle; then he sat down in the pleasant shade of a walnut tree. Now, the Hoca's mind was seldom idle, and while he relaxed for a few minutes in the shade, he meditated upon the great wisdom of Allah. Chancing to note a fine watermelon in the garden, he smiled to himself. "Now *there*," said he, "is something I'd have done differently had I been Allah. See that great, lovely watermelon growing on a spindly little vine, and then consider the walnut, a midget nut upon a great and lordly tree. Ah, who can fathom the wisdom of Allah? If *I* had been arranging matters, I should have given the walnuts to that puny vine, and reserved the watermelons for this magnificent tree." So musing, he nodded off for a nap.

Suddenly a walnut fell from the tree and landed with a substantial thump on the top of the Hoca's bald head. Awakened, the Hoca ruefully rubbed the lump which had begun to swell on his scalp. Then an understanding smile spread over his face. In due reverence, he fell to his knees.

"Oh, Allah!" he murmured, "forgive me my presumption. Thy wisdom is indeed great. Suppose *I* had been arranging matters? I should just now have been hit upon the head by a *watermelon*. Ah, Allah, great indeed is Thy wisdom!"

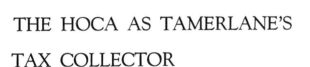

THE HOCA AS TAMERLANE'S
TAX COLLECTOR

ONE day the Hoca chanced to be in Tamerlane's court when the despot's tax collector came to report on his receipts. The figures in impressive columns covered page after page of parchment, and the collector's voice droned endlessly through a recital of the sums. But, in the end, Tamerlane was not satisfied. It seems that first this account and then that one had been misrepresented. In short, the tax collector had revealed himself as a scamp and a cheat.

29

"So *that* is the way you manage your post as tax collector!" raged the testy ruler. "Well, sir, I cannot swallow such outrageous lies. But"— and his eyes glinted—"*you* will swallow them. Begin at once!"

"Begin *what*, sire?" questioned the tax collector, puzzled and frightened.

"Begin to *swallow* your own accounts. Quickly, now. I have other business at hand." And the lordly Tamerlane watched with increasing amusement as the wretched collector choked and gagged on the sheets of parchment. At length he had chewed and swallowed them all, and his heroic effort was rewarded on the instant by Tamerlane, who declared him no longer tax collector.

"Instead," declared Tamerlane, smiling broadly, "I appoint *you*, Nasreddin Hoca, to be my tax collector."

Appalled, the Hoca considered his sad plight. There was little doubt about the matter: no report could please Tamerlane. On the other hand, was it necessary to suffer such abuse for one's bookkeeping, however faulty? Suddenly the Hoca had a fine idea. This business might be managed, after all . . . Gravely he thanked Tamerlane for his fine evidence of trust in a simple hoca's judgment, and excused himself from the ruler's presence, to prepare himself for his new office.

Every morning during the following month, Nasreddin Hoca watched with tender concern as his wife rolled fine, fresh dough to paper thinness (*yufka*) and baked it to form platelike pastries. Then he took the pastries to one side and on them he recorded the tax receipts of the preceding day. With painstaking care he stacked the pastries in a special cupboard where they would be protected from prying eye and tampering touch.

Finally came the day of reckoning. Taking a large wheelbarrow loaded with the precious pastries, the Hoca trundled off to Tamerlane's court, and was admitted to the ruler's presence with his curious burden.

"Ah, there you are!" exclaimed Tamerlane, slapping his hands on his knees in great satisfaction. And, "Yes, yes," he murmured as he accepted the two large leather sacks containing the taxes collected. "But where are your accounts?"

"Right here, sire," replied the Hoca, gesturing toward the load in the wheelbarrow.

Tamerlane stared in disbelief. Then, "Bring me one of those things," he demanded.

Promptly the Hoca presented him with one of the pastries, covered from end to end with finely penned figures. As Tamerlane studied the inscriptions, a smile began to spread across his face. "And *what*, may I ask, was your purpose in keeping your records on pastry?"

"Only, sire, that *either one* of us might be able to swallow the reports of my labors," answered the Hoca.

THE *SOUND* IS YOURS

ONE day as Nasreddin Hoca was walking through the forest, he came upon a peasant cutting wood. It was hard, heavy work, and every blow of the ax on the wood took all the force the peasant could muster. As the Hoca watched, he heard someone saying "*Hunh!*" every time the ax came down on the wood. There on a log sat the woodcutter's companion. And faithfully, with every blow he said "*Hunh!*" The Hoca wondered at this, but he went on his way without saying anything.

35

In a few days, the peasant went to the bazaar with his load of wood and sold it for a fair sum in coins. As he slipped the sack of coins into the pocket of his baggy trousers, his companion rushed up. "Half of that money is mine!" he insisted. "I did half of the work."

Astonished, the woodcutter debated the matter. Clearly, this was a case to be brought before the judge. Accordingly, the two went before the Hoca, who served the village as judge. Carefully the Hoca listened to both sides of the case. Then, calling the woodcutter to him, he directed him to lay the bag of coins on a flat stone. One by one, the Hoca dropped the coins on the stone. As they rang out with a pleasant jingle, he said to the companion, "Do you hear this?"

"Yes," the companion answered.

"Fine," said the Hoca. "The *sound* is yours, and the *coin* is the woodcutter's."

When the coins had all been sounded and turned over to the woodcutter, the Hoca dismissed the case.

In Turkey, a "straw boss" or "sidewalk superintend-ent" is known as "the woodcutter's hunh-sayer."

36

THE HOCA AND THE CANDLE

 ONE day during a particularly bitter winter, the Hoca and his friends sat in the coffeehouse discussing the weather. Plain talk gave way to boasting, and before long the Hoca puffed out his chest importantly. "You may think we are having a cold winter. As for me, I thrive on cold and snow. Why, when I was a boy, I used to go out in the middle of January and break the ice on the river so that I could have a good, brisk swim for myself. Pooh! This cold is *nothing*."

This claim was too exaggerated for the rest of them. Nudging a companion, the Hoca's best friend set out a fine challenge. "I say, Hoca. You like cold weather. I suppose you could stay out all night long in the cold without a coat or a blanket and nothing at all to warm yourself?"

"Of course," bragged the Hoca.

"No fire, no hot tea, no blanket, no coat?" The others seemed impressed.

"Well," said the ringleader, "we'll make a bargain with you. If tonight you can stay outside, with absolutely nothing extra to warm you, all night long, you'll be our guest at a fine dinner. Right, friends?"

"Right!" they chorused.

"On the other hand," the ringleader continued, "if you use any means at all of keeping yourself warm, you will entertain us for dinner. How about that, Hoca *effendi?*"

"Fine, fine," agreed the Hoca.

That evening the Hoca's friends watched through the windows of their warm houses as the Hoca strolled here and there, studying the stars in the chill sky, and repenting a thousand times of his hasty, boastful tongue. Just as he was about to concede

38

defeat, he spied a candle set in a window perhaps a hundred meters away. Fixing his eye on the candle glow, the Hoca felt the blood flow back through his stiffening veins. Thus he was able to endure the long night.

The next morning his friends, stepping outside into the frosty air, were amazed to find the Hoca calm and smiling, none the worse for his chill vigil. "Well, Hoca *effendi,* are you *sure* you used no means at all of warming yourself?" persisted the ringleader.

"No means at all," the Hoca declared, "unless you can call a candle a hundred meters away a means! I *did* see a candle burning, and its glow kept me equal to the torments of the cold."

"Aha!" exclaimed the challenger. "Hoca *effendi*, you must be our host at dinner, for you warmed yourself by that candle." No protest on the part of the Hoca was sufficient to move the resolve of his friends on the matter, so they were invited that evening to dinner at the Hoca's house.

The group arrived in good time, and sat on bolsters in the Hoca's sparsely furnished living room, waiting for the delicious smells that must herald a fine meal. But, sniff as they would, they could detect not a hint of what was to be served for dinner. What's more, the Hoca kept excusing himself to go out to the kitchen and supervise the cooking, a most unusual procedure for him. As one hour succeeded another with still no sign of food, the men

40

began to grumble among themselves, and at last the ringleader chaffed the Hoca about the delay.

"Ah, my friends, you can come and see for yourselves that your dinner is being made ready," declared their host, and he led the way to the kitchen. Following him, they were amazed to find a large caldron suspended from the ceiling. A meter below the caldron burned a single candle.

"But, Hoca *effendi*," spluttered the ringleader, "surely you don't expect to heat that caldron with a *candle*? Why, the dinner would *never* get done!"

"Oh, I'm not so sure," answered the Hoca calmly. "If a candle a *hundred* meters away can keep me warm all night long, surely a candle one meter away can heat a caldron!"

THE HOCA SOLVES A PROBLEM

ONE day as the Hoca was strolling along the river, he heard a cry for help. Hurrying along the shore, the Hoca came to a group of his students splashing in the water after a good swim.

"Oh, Hoca *effendi*," called one of the boys, "we need your help. It is time for us to go home for lunch, but we cannot get out of the water."

"And why not?" asked the Hoca.

"Well, Hoca *effendi*, when we came in to swim, each boy had his own legs. But we have been in so long that our legs are all mixed up. We cannot tell which legs are which. Please, Hoca *effendi*, come in and help us!" And the boys grinned at each other, waiting to see how their teacher would solve this interesting dilemma.

The Hoca thought for a moment. Then he walked to a small willow tree and cut a supple switch. Carrying it to the edge of the river, he began to use it most effectively indeed on the arms and shoulders of the boys. Hastily one after another they clambered up the bank.

"There, now," smiled the Hoca when the last of the boys had come ashore. "You found your own legs, after all!"

THE HOCA AND ALLAH'S SON-IN-LAW

ONE evening as the Hoca was about to go to bed, there came a loud knock at the door. Answering the knock, the Hoca found on the doorstep a wretched-looking beggar. "Alms!" croaked the visitor. "And not only alms, Hoca *effendi*, but shelter on this dreary night. I am Allah's own son-in-law. For the sake of Allah, give me shelter."

"Allah's *son-in-law?*" inquired the Hoca, scarcely believing his ears.

"You have heard," answered the beggar.

"Ah, yes," the Hoca replied. "I have excellent quarters for you. But please wait a moment until I put on my coat."

Puzzled, the petitioner waited on the doorstep while the Hoca secured his coat. Then, stepping briskly ahead of the beggar, the Hoca took him through one winding street after another, until the two stood at last before the mosque.

"Here you are," said the Hoca. "You will surely feel more at home in your father-in-law's house than you would in mine!"

NASREDDIN HOCA AND THE THIRD SHOT

ONE day as Nasreddin Hoca was chatting with the Emperor Tamerlane, he chanced to see archers practicing in a nearby field. "Ha! So *those* are your archers!" he exclaimed. And a reminiscent gleam came into his eye. "Not an archer in that whole field can shoot as well as I," he boasted. "In my youth, I was champion archer of this whole area of Turkey."

"Hmm," murmured Tamerlane. "Champion, eh? Well, if you were champion, you can certainly teach my men something. Come along. I was just about to ride out and inspect the practice."

46

At this, the Hoca began to tremble. In truth, he was no archer at all, and never had been. But to boast before the great Tamerlane and then fail to make good on one's boast could be a very expensive mistake. Deeply regretting his rash statement, the Hoca mounted his little gray donkey and trotted out after the Emperor to the field.

Calling his men to him, Tamerlane bade them attend closely, for they were to receive an archery lesson from a real champion. The Hoca was then given a bow and three arrows, and motioned to position.

In an effort to gain time, the Hoca gravely studied the target. By Allah, he could barely *see* it! He shook his head thoughtfully. "If I had only remembered to practice what I so often preach to my students: 'Listen a hundred times; ponder a thousand times; speak once'!" he mourned.

But Tamerlane was becoming impatient, and well the Hoca knew the cost of further delay. He could do no more than try . . . Taking careful aim, the Hoca released the first arrow. It wavered, and fell just a short distance ahead of him. The Hoca smiled confidently. "*That*, sire, is the way your captains shoot."

With even greater care, the Hoca placed and aimed the second arrow. Alas, it traveled very little farther than the first one. Here and there among the archers a chuckle was heard, speedily silenced by the baleful glance of Tamerlane. But the Hoca beamed, and proclaimed, *"That,* sire, is how your generals shoot."

With infinite care, the Hoca fitted the third arrow to the string. Calmly he spat to ward off the evil eye. Then he aimed the arrow. Allah help him, the bow slipped in his trembling hand, and the arrow, released with surprising force, flew straight to its goal, lodging itself neatly exactly in the center of the target.

The Hoca, much cleverer with his wits than with his hands, looked about him proudly. "And *that,* sire, is how your humble servant Nasreddin Hoca used to shoot when he was archery champion!"

I KNOW WHAT *I'LL* DO

ONE day the Hoca fell asleep as he was jogging along the road on his little gray donkey. Seeing a fine chance for a joke, several of his students slipped up behind him and removed the worn saddlebag from his donkey's back. Then they waited to see what would happen.

49

When he arrived at his stable door, the Hoca dismounted and reached out to remove the saddlebag. To his astonishment, it had disappeared entirely. The Hoca rubbed his eyes and looked again, but the saddlebag was nowhere to be seen.

The next day he encountered several of his students on the street that ran past the public fountain. "Boys," said he, "my saddlebag is gone. If you don't bring it back to me, I know what *I'll* do . . ." and he muttered something under his breath.

The boys looked at one another in dismay. Their prank had suddenly become a serious matter. In no time at all, they brought the missing saddlebag and presented it to the Hoca.

Thanking them, the Hoca installed it in its rightful place on the back of his little donkey, and he was about to ride away when one of the boys could contain his curiosity no longer. "I say, Hoca *effendi*," he began, "what were you going to do if we did not return the saddlebag?"

"Ah," answered the Hoca mildly, "I have at home a piece of old carpet. If you had not returned the saddlebag, I should have had to make another one."

50

EAT, MY FINE COAT!

 ONE day the Hoca was invited to a banquet at the home of the *muhtar*, the most important man in the town of Akshehir. All day as he worked in his vineyard, he thought with relish of the fine food and the good conversation ahead of him. But, alas, he had misjudged his day's work, and he arrived home with too little time to dress with the particular care needed for such a grand occasion. It was either not wash and dress or be late for dinner, and he must on no account be late for dinner, so off he went in his workaday dress and with the marks of his day's toil upon his hands and face.

When he arrived at the *muhtar's* door, the rest of the guests had already come, and conversations buzzed around the room. Curiously enough, no one asked the Hoca's opinion on any matter, though at other banquets he had been the one most solicited for comment and advice. The *muhtar* himself scarcely noticed him. And when the time came for the guests to be seated for dinner, the Hoca was placed in the spot farthest removed from his host.

Quietly the neglected guest excused himself from the group and hurried home. There he scrubbed himself from bald head to heels. Next, he attired himself handsomely in his new baggy trousers, an elegant shirt and vest, and his largest turban. Then he slipped into his new fur coat, by far the most striking garment in all Akshehir. At last he was ready.

With his head held high, he presented himself again at the *muhtar's* door. Every eye was upon him as the servants admitted him to the house. Rising immediately, the host came to greet him, and led him straight to the place of honor at his own tray. As the dinner progressed, the *muhtar* addressed one question after another to his learned guest, and served him the finest foods as soon as they were brought in by the servants. But to the *muhtar's* astonishment, the Hoca began stuffing first one food and then another into the generous pockets of his new coat. "Eat, my fine coat!" he would say each time he tucked another handful of food into the pockets. "Eat, my fine coat!"

First the *muhtar* watched; then everyone watched, but no one could make any sense of the Hoca's strange behavior. Finally the *muhtar* could remain silent no longer about the matter. "Hoca, *effendi*," said he, "what *are* you doing?"

"Ah, sire, I am but feeding the guest you invited to the banquet. When I came the first time this evening, you gave me no notice at all; when I came the second time, you treated me as the guest of honor. *I* have not changed; I am still Nasreddin Hoca. Therefore it must be my fur coat to which you are giving such honor. Since my coat is the guest of honor, it should have a fair share of this fine food!"

COW OR DONKEY?

ONE day shortly after the Hoca had married, his wife came to him to ask that he buy a cow, so that they might have milk in the house.

"My dear," replied the Hoca, "I'd be happy to buy you a cow if we had a bigger stable. But our stable is just large enough for my little donkey. You can see that he would be crowded if we bought a cow. I want him to be comfortable."

This seemed scarcely reason enough to do without a cow, so day after day his wife repeated her request, until at last the Hoca could deny her no longer. Mounting his little donkey, he rode to the market-place and, after a whole morning's thought and bargaining, he selected a cow and led her home.

Still certain that his donkey would suffer, the Hoca took care to acquaint Allah with his problem. Kneeling and touching his forehead reverently to his prayer rug, the Hoca then turned palms up in appeal. "Oh, Allah!" he prayed. "Thou knowest that I love my little donkey, and that he will not be comfortable with this new cow sharing his stable. Oh, Allah, if it be Thy will, take the life of the new cow, that my little donkey may be at peace!" Having placed his worry in the hands of Allah, the Hoca went about his business.

The next morning the Hoca hurried out to the stable to see how his donkey had fared. But to his amazement, he found his little donkey dead. "*Ey, vah! Ey, vah!*" the Hoca wailed, struck to the heart with grief.

The Hoca's wife, hearing him cry out, ran to the window. "Hoca, Hoca! Are you sick?" she called.

"No, no, wife," replied the Hoca. "It is nothing."
And his wife returned to her work.

"No," added the Hoca under his breath, bitterly,
"it is nothing but my little donkey!" And as soon as
his wife had left the window, the Hoca fell to his
knees. Hands extended palms up in appeal, he cried
out, "Ah, Allah! Thou art great and good and all-
wise. Canst Thou not tell the difference between a
cow and a *donkey?*"

NASREDDIN MINDS THE DOOR

ONE day when Nasreddin Hoca was just a boy, his mother decided to take the family clothes down to the river for a good washing. But how was she to mind the house while she was gone? Of course, there was young Nasreddin, and he usually managed to do what he was told . . .

"Nasreddin," she called, "I am going down to the river to wash our clothes, and I shall not be back for an hour or so. Please keep a good eye on the door while I am gone."

58

"Yes, Mother," the boy agreed, and for the first hour or so he was content enough, inside the house, outside the house, always in sight of the door. But after the second hour had passed, and then another, he became tired of such close quarters, and he decided to go down to the river to see what could be keeping his mother.

Since his mother had told him to keep a good eye on the door, however, Nasreddin could scarcely go. Or *could* he? In a matter of moments, he had removed the door from its hinges and hoisted it onto his back. Off he went toward the river.

As soon as he came into sight, his mother cried out, "Nasreddin, what are you doing here? I thought I had left you to mind the door?"

"Oh, don't worry, Mother," he answered cheerfully. "I brought the door!"

HOW LONG WILL IT TAKE?

ONE afternoon the Hoca was resting at the edge of his vineyard before starting back to the village for his dinner. Along the dusty road came a traveler, a stranger to that neighborhood.

"I say, Hoca *effendi*, how long will it take me to walk to the next village?" the stranger asked.

Nasreddin Hoca studied the traveler quietly, but he did not answer.

Puzzled, the stranger muttered to himself, "Well, the fellow is either stupid or deaf! I'll ask him again."

"I say, Hoca *effendi*," he repeated more loudly, "how long will it take me to walk to the next village?"

Nasreddin Hoca thought the matter over, but he still did not answer.

Irritated, the stranger shouted, "I say, Hoca *effendi*, how long will it take me to walk to the next village?"

As Nasreddin Hoca still made no reply, the traveler turned away angrily and began to walk with great strides toward the village. After watching him for a minute or two, the Hoca called, "My friend, it will take you no longer than fifteen minutes."

Surprised, the stranger turned around. "Well, why didn't you tell me that before?" he exclaimed.

"How could I say," answered the Hoca calmly, "until I knew how fast you planned to walk?"

A DONKEY TRANSFORMED

ONE day the Hoca, desiring to buy an agreeable donkey to set a good example for the bad-tempered one in his own stable, rode to the village market. After carefully examining the donkeys for sale, he chose a mild-mannered little beast with four sturdy legs and, placing a halter around its neck, he led it behind him as he rode his old donkey back home.

Noting that the Hoca was nodding sleepily as he rode, two scamps slipped up to the new donkey. One removed the halter from the donkey's neck and placed it around his own neck; the other quietly led the donkey back to the marketplace, where he obtained a good price for it.

The Hoca awoke as his donkey stopped at the door of his own stable, and turned to survey his new purchase. To his surprise, the agreeable little donkey had disappeared, and in its place was a ragged boy, with the donkey's halter snugly around his neck.

"What's this!" exclaimed the Hoca. "Where is my new donkey?"

The boy hung his head. "I was your new donkey, Hoca *effendi*. You see, I have always been a stubborn and disobedient boy, and my mother one day became so disgusted with me that she asked Allah to change me into the donkey I must surely be. Suddenly I had four legs and long ears, and a donkey I would have remained if it had not been for your kind heart in choosing me today. Thank you so much, Hoca *effendi*. Now may I return to my mother?"

63

Still shaking his head in bewilderment, the Hoca removed the halter from the boy's neck and, cautioning him this time to *behave* himself, the Hoca sent him home.

Then, since he still needed a new donkey, the Hoca rode back to the marketplace. There, to his surprise, he found the same mild-mannered little donkey waiting to be sold.

Hastily dismounting, the Hoca hurried over to the beast and whispered in his ear, "You naughty boy! Will you *never* learn your lesson?"

IT'S ALL IN KNOWING HOW

ONE day the Hoca went with a group of friends for a picnic along a little river near the village. While some of the group set out the food for the meal, the Hoca and three or five others removed their outer clothing and splashed about in the cool water. Suddenly a great splash was heard, followed by a loud cry and then an ominous silence.

"It's the tax collector!" shouted the Hoca. "He has fallen into the water."

"But he cannot swim!" Quickly the *beckche,* the village watchman, swam toward the spot where the tax collector had last been seen. As soon as the tax collector's head appeared again above the water, the *beckche* called, "Give me your hand, and I'll pull you out."

"*Kuk-kuk-kuk,*" gurgled the tax collector, and under the water he sank.

Once more, as the tax collector's head appeared, the *beckche* cried, "Quick, quick, give me your hand so that I may save you!"

"*Kuk-kuk-kuk,*" gurgled the tax collector weakly, and down he sank.

For the third time the head appeared above the water, with a "*Kuk-kuk-kuk!*" Just as the drowning man began to sink again, the Hoca cried, "Take my hand!" Immediately the tax collector reached out, and the Hoca pulled him ashore.

As soon as the tax collector had gasped and recovered his breath, the others crowded around the Hoca. "Tell us, Hoca. How could *you* manage to save him when the *beckche* couldn't?"

"It's all in knowing how," the Hoca said gravely. "The tax collector is a man who has *taken* all his life; he would not willingly *give anything,* even his hand to save himself from drowning!"

IT WON'T DO YOU ANY GOOD

 ONE day the Hoca was greatly pleased with a fine dish of liver and lungs served to him at the home of a friend. Wishing to have his own wife prepare the dish for him at home, the Hoca asked for the recipe, and his friend's wife was only too happy to oblige him.

On the way home, the Hoca stopped in at the butcher's and bought two kilos of nice, fresh liver and lungs. Tucking the recipe safely into the pocket of his baggy trousers, and swinging the packet of meat at the end of a stout string, the Hoca set off for his house.

Suddenly a large crow swooped down, snatched the parcel, and flew off with it. But the Hoca caught sight of him in time to have the last word. "Take it, then, but it won't do you any good. *I* have the recipe!"

BOILED WHEAT FOR A
BOUNTIFUL HARVEST

NE day a poor traveler chanced to find himself in Akshehir without so much as a *kurus* in his pockets. Feeling very hungry, he went boldly into a restaurant, sat down, and ordered two boiled eggs, bread, and tea. He ate with immense satisfaction and then, waiting until the restaurant owner's back was turned, he slipped out without paying for his meal.

As it happened, he later found work as a porter, settled down in Akshehir, and, by dint of hard labor and good management, succeeded after a year or so in saving a considerable sum of money. Desiring to square his overdue account with the restaurant owner, he went to him and reminded him of the occasion on which he had slipped out of the restaurant without paying his bill. "I have come today," he concluded, "to pay you for that meal. Not only that, but I intend to pay you *double*. Now, let's see. The eggs would be about 50 *kurus* apiece; the bread would at most cost 25 *kurus*; the tea would cost 15 or 20 *kurus*. We'll round it off to 200 *kurus*, or two *liras*. I'd like to pay you four *liras*." And he held out four shiny *lira* pieces to the restaurant owner.

But the restaurant owner had been eyeing the fellow closely. He appeared prosperous, indeed. Why should he pay a mere four *liras* when he could obviously pay much more?

"Ah, ah! Not so fast, my friend," said the proprietor. "Just think for a moment. If I had not served you those two eggs, the eggs could have produced two chickens; each of those chickens would have laid a great many eggs by now, and each of those eggs would have hatched a chicken. You owe me *far more* than four *liras*. Come, I shall settle for 100 *liras*."

"*One hundred!*" the debtor exclaimed. "Indeed, you will get no such sum from me. In fact, now you may count yourself fortunate to get the two *liras* I truly owe you!" He slapped the two coins down on the counter and turned to leave.

"Stop, thief!" called the proprietor, and, summoning a *gendarme*, he had the debtor taken before the judge.

Now, Nasreddin Hoca had been sitting in the restaurant while the two had been talking, and he had listened with great interest. Just as the poor fellow was being hauled away, the Hoca stepped up to him and said, "Don't worry, *effendi*. I heard the whole thing, and I shall be glad to witness for you in court tomorrow."

But the next day, the Hoca was nowhere to be found. Time after time, the judge postponed the case of the overdue bill and went on to other things, confident that the Hoca would shortly make his appearance as witness. Finally, however, all the rest of the cases on the docket had been heard and disposed of, and the Hoca still had not come. Greatly annoyed, the judge sent a messenger to the Hoca's house after him. Almost an hour passed before the messenger reappeared, bringing the Hoca.

"Well!" exclaimed the judge. "You had business in court today, Hoca *effendi*. What were you doing that was more important than appearing in court?"

"Sire," responded the Hoca, "this morning as my wife was boiling wheat for our breakfast, it occurred to me that eating the wheat would be wasting it. Just think how many kilos of wheat could be raised from just that handful of boiled wheat! 'Better to plant this boiled wheat than to eat it,' I said to my wife. 'Then we shall never need to fear hunger, for we shall have a bountiful harvest to lean upon.' She agreed with me, so as soon as the wheat was thoroughly boiled, I took it out to the field to plant it. Your messenger found me there. Now, if you will excuse me, I still have a row or so to plant before I am done." And the Hoca turned to go.

"Wait!" shouted the judge. He stared at the Hoca. "Did you say you were planting *boiled* wheat? Why, Hoca *effendi*, even a child knows that boiled wheat will not grow to produce anything but disappointment. Whatever made you think of planting boiled wheat?"

"Well, sire," the Hoca replied, his sober speech belying the twinkle in his eye, "as I was thinking over the case for which I was to be witness today, it occurred to me that if boiled eggs could produce chickens, boiled wheat could surely produce a bountiful crop!"

Suddenly the whole court sensed the ridiculousness of the restaurant owner's suit. "Case dismissed!" announced the judge, leaving the proprietor no more than his rightful two *liras* for the traveler's meal.